MARK TEAGUE
FUNNY FARM

SCHOLASTIC INC.
New York Toronto London Auckland
Sydney Mexico City New Delhi Hong Kong

For Laura

ISBN: 978-0-545-20960-1

Text and illustrations copyright © 2009 by Mark Teague.
All rights reserved. Published by Orchard Books, an imprint of Scholastic Inc. ORCHARD BOOKS and design are registered trademarks of Watts Publishing Group, Ltd., used under license. SCHOLASTIC and associated logos are trademarks and/or registered trademarks of Scholastic Inc.

12 11 10 9 8 7 6 5 4 3 2 1   10 11 12 13 14 15/0

Printed in the U.S.A.   08

First Scholastic paperback printing, February 2010

The artwork was created in oil paints.
The book was set in 20-point Eagle Book.
Book design by Charles Kreloff

In the spring, Cousin Judy, Uncle Earl, and Aunt Josephine meet Edward at the station.

It is Edward's first visit to Hawthorne Farm.

In the morning, everyone gets up early.

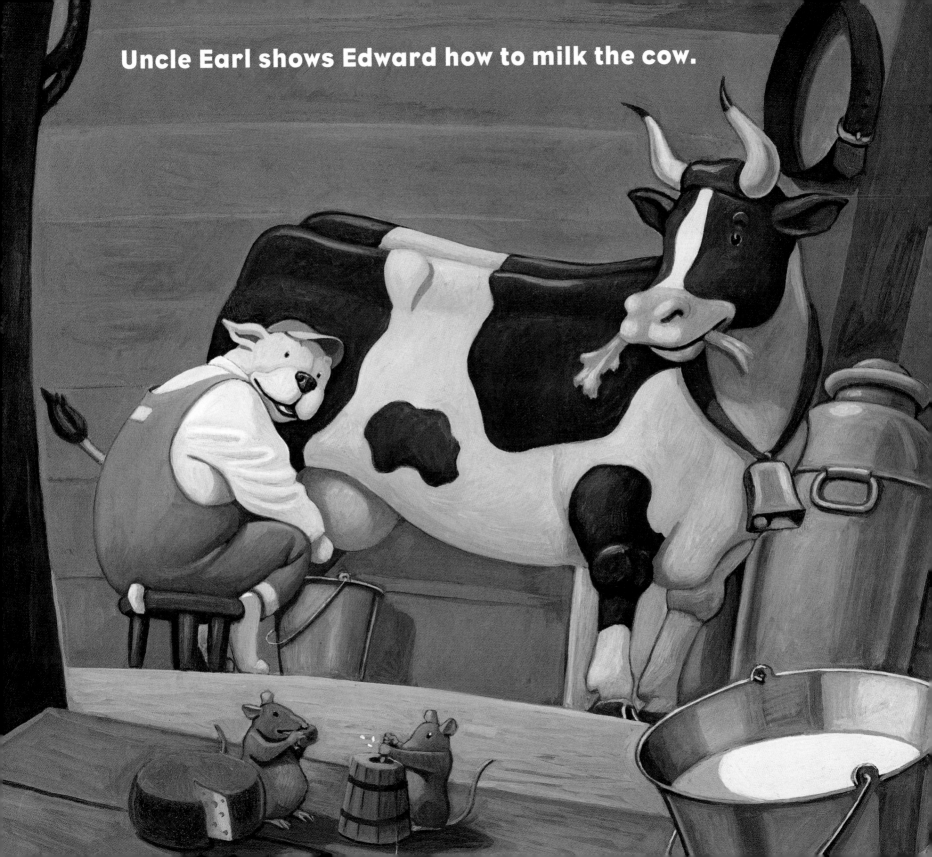

Uncle Earl shows Edward how to milk the cow.

Judy helps Edward feed the pigs.

Edward gathers eggs from the henhouse.

In the woods, Edward helps make maple syrup.

Uncle Earl plows the field.

Edward digs a hole in the garden.

When it rains, Edward goes inside.

Judy teaches Edward how to knit.

Edward and Judy go outside to tend the sheep.

Before supper, Edward paints the barn.

Edward is very hungry at dinner.

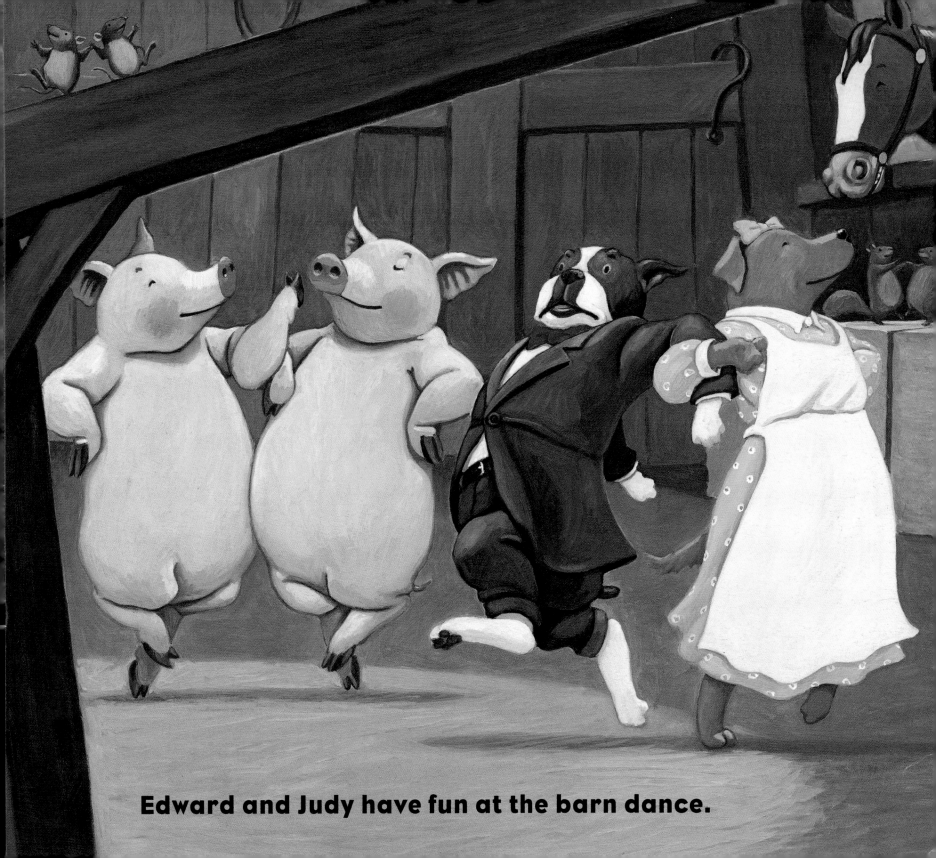

Edward and Judy have fun at the barn dance.

It is bedtime at Hawthorne Farm.